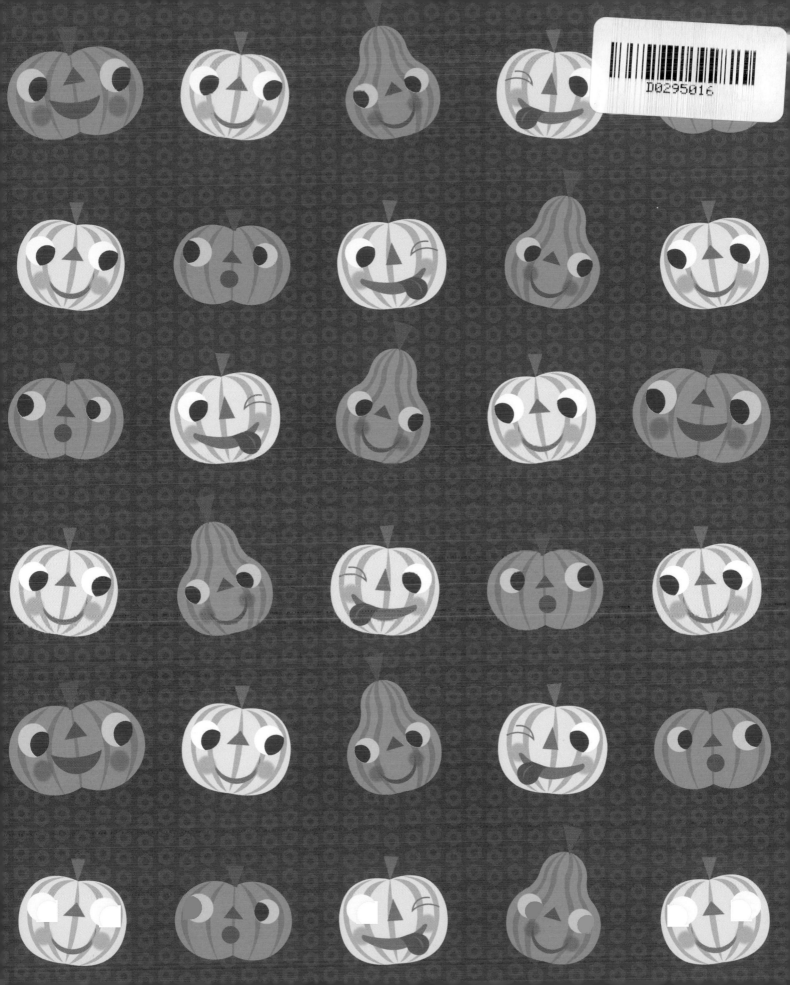

A SPOOKTACULAR
PLACE TO BE

A SPOOKTACULAR PLACE TO BE

ÚNA WOODS

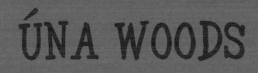

THE O'BRIEN PRESS
DUBLIN

In his moon-shaped park filled with silver moonlight,
The Dublin Vampire wakes to the same familiar sight.

'I've spent so many years in this creepy old tree,
Is there a more spooktacular place to be?'

He agrees with his bat that it's time to explore,

'Let's go on an all-Ireland ghost bus tour!'

'All aboard!' They get comfortable up in their seats
As the bus rumbles off through the dark city streets.

At St Michan's Church, in an underground room,
Ancient mummies have fun in their old stone tomb.

8

'It's way too far down, it's too deep for me.

Is there a more spooktacular place to be?'

In Loftus Hall, ghosts of old ladies and lords

Swish past the old curtains and creaky floorboards.

'Achoooooo! This old house is too dusty for me.

Is there a more spooktacular place to be?'

WEEEEEEEEEEEE

At Fastnet lighthouse, the Banshee flashes the big light.

With big waves crashing round, it's a hair-raising sight.

'But it makes me feel dizzy; it's too high for me.

Is there a more spooktacular place to be?'

At Leap Castle, the Red Lady glides round the halls
and phantoms float through the magnificent walls.

'But my pet bat's not allowed in here with me.

Is there a more spooktacular place to be?'

Out on Skellig Michael, an old witch of stone
Stands wailing and crying out there on her own.

'This wind is too bitter and chilly for me.

Is there a more spooktacular place to be?'

In the Aillwee Caves a load of bats play.

They can see even though it's so dark all day.

'Well, one bat's quite enough for me!

Is there a more spooktacular place to be?'

Awwwooooo!

In Hazelwood forest, out under the moon,

The Púca is singing his loud, eerie tune.

AWOOOOOOOO!! 'That music's a bit much for me.

Is there a more spooktacular place to be?'

At Newgrange, skeletons rattle their bones;
They dance before dawn in their Stone Age home

22

'This space is just too small for me.

Is there a more spooktacular place to be?'

In Donegal, ghost pirates laugh and play tricks.

Their shipwreck would make you a little seasick.

'This cold, choppy ocean is too rough for me.

Is there a more spooktacular place to be?'

These pumpkins look ready for Halloween night
When their spooky faces will give folks a fright.

'It reminds me of somewhere that I long to be,
The most spooktacular place in the whole country.'

The Ghost Bus heads off over valleys and hills,

Through old creepy forests that would give you the chills

'Those sights will take some beating, that's for sure,
But where is the final stop on our tour?'

'My own moon-shaped park, right down by the sea!

Oh, it's good to be home in my creepy old tree.

With all my new friends here, I think you'll agree,

This is the most spooktacular place to be.'

To Barna

Úna Woods is an illustrator and author who lives in Dublin. She loves making illustrations for children and her work has been published in books, magazines and websites.

She loves working with bright colours and patterns in her illustrations. She grew up in Clontarf, very close to where Bram Stoker was born.

Úna is the author and illustrator of *Have You Seen the Dublin Vampire?*
www.unawoods.com

First published 2021 by The O'Brien Press Ltd,
12 Terenure Road East, Rathgar, Dublin 6, D06 HD27, Ireland
Tel: +353 1 4923333; Fax: +353 1 4922777
E-mail: books@obrien.ie
Website: www.obrien.ie
The O'Brien Press is a member of Publishing Ireland.

Published in

DUBLIN
UNESCO
City of Literature

ISBN: 978-1-78849-285-0

6 5 4 3 2 1
23 22 21

Printed and bound in Poland by Białostockie Zakłady Graficzne S.A.
The paper in this book is produced using pulp from managed forests.